Lets Go, White Sox™!

DISCARD

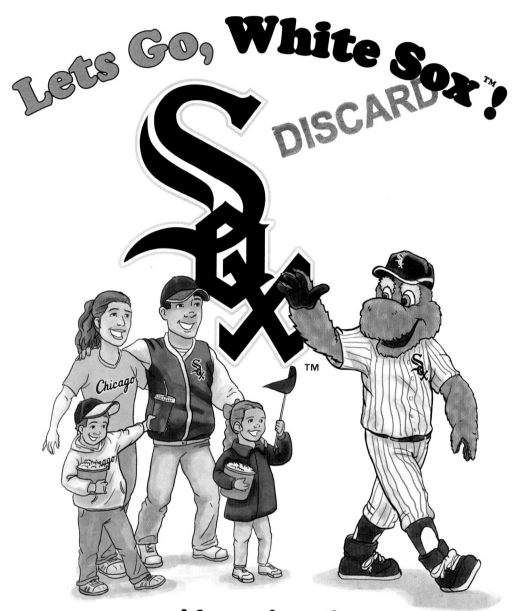

Aimee Aryal

Illustrated by M. De Angel with D. Moore

MASCOT BOOKS®

www.mascotbooks.com

It was a beautiful day for baseball on Chicago's South Side. *Chicago White Sox* fans from all over the area were on their way to the ballpark.

Southpaw™, the Chicago White Sox mascot, joined many *White Sox* fans aboard the "L" train. As they arrived at the stadium station, fans cheered, "Let's go, White Sox!"

Ready for the game, White Sox fans
walked from the train station to the
ballpark. Everyone was excited about
seeing the home team in action.

A father and son waved to
Southpaw and cheered,
"Let's go, White Sox!"

It was now time for batting practice. The team was dressed in their black practice jerseys. Each player took a turn in the batting cage.

After receiving a few helpful batting tips
from Southpaw, a player hit several
balls out of the park. The player said,
"Let's go, White Sox!"

After batting practice, the ballpark grounds crew went to work. With great pride, they quickly prepared the field for play.

One man wheeled away the batting cage,
while another man raked the infield.
As the grounds crew worked, they cheered
"Let's go, White Sox!"

White Sox fans made their way to
the concession stands. One family
stopped for peanuts, popcorn,
and a White Sox pennant.

As the family headed back to
their seats, they cheered,
"Let's go, White Sox!"

It was now time to meet the White Sox
players. As each player was announced,
they ran out of the dugout and stood on
the third base line.

Southpaw walked down the third base line
and greeted each player with a high-five.
The players said, "Let's go, White Sox!"

The umpire yelled, "PLAY BALL!"
and a batter stepped to the plate.
It was time for the first pitch.

The White Sox pitcher stepped on the pitcher's mound and delivered a perfect fastball. The umpire called, "STRIKE ONE!" The game was underway!

There was a festive atmosphere in the
ballpark as White Sox fans were enjoying
a great day of baseball and fun.

One family stood up and
started a White Sox cheer. They
yelled, "Let's go, White Sox!"

It was now time for the seventh inning
stretch and the singing of
Take Me Out To The Ballgame™!

Southpaw invited some of his closest friends
to join him on top of the White Sox dugout as
he led the crowd in song. Afterwards, White
Sox fans cheered, "Let's go, White Sox!"

With the game tied in the bottom of the ninth inning, a White Sox player hit a deep fly ball over the right field fence. HOME RUN!

Several fans tried to catch the
home run ball. The crowd cheered,
"White Sox win! White Sox win!"

Everyone celebrated the thrilling White Sox victory. After the game, fans walked through the parking lot and made their way back to the train station.

Once Southpaw returned home, he
crawled into bed and thought about all
the fun he had at the ballpark.
Let's go, White Sox!

Entertaining is what mascots do best, so let *Southpaw*™, the *Chicago White Sox*™ mascot, be a big hit at your next event. Birthday parties, in-game visits, school assemblies, graduations, store openings, parades, weddings, and more.

For details about booking *Southpaw*™ to attend your next party or event call (312) 674-5312 or visit www.whitesox.com/southpaw

Hey Kids! Don't forget to sign up for the White Sox Kids Club, presented by Pepsi.

For more information call (312) 674-5504 or visit www.whitesox.com

For Maya and Anna. ~ Aimee Aryal
For Sue, Ana Milagros, and Angel Miguel. ~ Miguel De Angel

For more information about our products,
please visit us online at www.mascotbooks.com.

Mascot Books, Inc. - P.O. Box 220157, Chantilly, VA 20153-0157

Major League Baseball trademarks and copyrights are used
with permission of Major League Baseball Properties, Inc. MLB.com

ISBN: 978-1-932888-87-4
Printed in the United States.
www.mascotbooks.com

Let Cort the Sport™ teach your children about good sportsmanship
www.mascotbooks.com

Meet Cort The Sport
The Little Eagles of Brookfield Elementary School meet Cort the Sport and Miss McCall for the first time. Read along as the children learn how to use Cort's Three Rules of Sportsmanship to transform another "Brookfield Blow-Up" into a great display of sportsmanship!

Cort Spells It Out
The Brookfield Elementary School Spelling Bee is only a week away, but why is one of the school's best spellers not going to enter the competition? Read along as Chip overcomes his nerves and discovers that Cort's Three Rules of Sportsmanship™ aren't just for sports.

Cort Reaches The Goal
Despite giving it his all, Tommy does not make the Brookfield Elementary School soccer team. Instead of hanging his head, Tommy decides to stay positive and practice even harder. Read along as Cort helps Tommy take advantage of his second chance on the soccer field.

Cort Plays The Part
The Brookfield Elementary School Play is right around the corner and Sammie dreams about being the star of the show. Find out how Sammie reacts when the leading role goes to another student. Cort teaches the Little Eagles what it means to act like a good sport.

MLB

Boston Red Sox™
Hello, Wally!
by Jerry Remy

*Wally And His Journey
Through Red Sox Nation™*
by Jerry Remy

New York Yankees™
Let's Go, Yankees™!
by Yogi Berra

New York Mets™
Hello, Mr. Met™!
by Rusty Staub

St. Louis Cardinals™
Hello, Fredbird™!
by Ozzie Smith

Chicago Cubs™
Let's Go, Cubs™!
by Aimee Aryal

Chicago White Sox™
Let's Go, White Sox™!
by Aimee Aryal

Philadelphia Phillies™
Hello, Phillie Phanatic™!
by Aimee Aryal

Cleveland Indians™
Hello, Slider™!
by Bob Feller

NBA

Dallas Mavericks
Let's Go, Mavs!
by Mark Cuban

NFL

Dallas Cowboys
How 'Bout Them Cowboys!
by Aimee Aryal

More Coming Soon

Collegiate

Auburn University
War Eagle! by Pat Dye
Hello, Aubie! by Aimee Aryal

Boston College
Hello, Baldwin! by Aimee Aryal

Brigham Young University
Hello, Cosmo!
by Pat and LaVell Edwards

Clemson University
Hello, Tiger! by Aimee Aryal

Duke University
Hello, Blue Devil! by Aimee Aryal

Florida State University
Let's Go 'Noles! by Aimee Aryal

Georgia Tech
Hello, Buzz! by Aimee Aryal

Indiana University
Let's Go Hoosiers! by Aimee Aryal

James Madison University
Hello, Duke Dog! by Aimee Aryal

Kansas State University
Hello, Willie! by Dan Walter

Louisiana State University
Hello, Mike! by Aimee Aryal

Michigan State University
Hello, Sparty! by Aimee Aryal

Mississippi State University
Hello, Bully! by Aimee Aryal

North Carolina State University
Hello, Mr. Wuf! by Aimee Aryal

Penn State University
We Are Penn State by Joe Paterno
Hello, Nittany Lion! by Aimee Aryal

Purdue University
Hello, Purdue Pete! by Aimee Aryal

Rutgers University
Hello, Scarlet Knight! by Aimee Aryal

Syracuse University
Hello, Otto! by Aimee Aryal

Texas A&M
Howdy, Reveille! by Aimee Aryal

UCLA
Hello, Joe Bruin! by Aimee Aryal

University of Alabama
Roll Tide! by Kenny Stabler
Hello, Big Al! by Aimee Aryal

University of Arkansas
Hello, Big Red! By Aimee Aryal

University of Connecticut
Hello, Jonathan! by Aimee Aryal

University of Florida
Hello, Albert! by Aimee Aryal

University of Georgia
How 'Bout Them Dawgs!
by Vince Dooley
Hello, Hairy Dawg! by Aimee Aryal

University of Illinois
Let's Go, Illini! by Aimee Aryal

University of Iowa
Hello, Herky! by Aimee Aryal

University of Kansas
Hello, Big Jay! by Aimee Aryal

University of Kentucky
Hello, Wildcat! by Aimee Aryal

University of Maryland
Hello, Testudo! by Aimee Aryal

University of Michigan
Let's Go, Blue! by Aimee Aryal

University of Minnesota
Hello, Goldy! by Aimee Aryal

University of Mississippi
Hello, Colonel Rebel! by Aimee Aryal

University of Nebraska
Hello, Herbie Husker! by Aimee Aryal

University of North Carolina
Hello, Rameses! by Aimee Aryal

University of Notre Dame
Let's Go Irish! by Aimee Aryal

University of Oklahoma
Let's Go Sooners! by Aimee Aryal

University of South Carolina
Hello, Cocky! by Aimee Aryal

University of Southern California
Hello, Tommy Trojan! by Aimee Aryal

University of Tennessee
Hello, Smokey! by Aimee Aryal

University of Texas
Hello, Hook 'Em! by Aimee Aryal

University of Virginia
Hello, CavMan! by Aimee Aryal

University of Wisconsin
Hello, Bucky! by Aimee Aryal

Virginia Tech
Yea, It's Hokie Game Day!
by Cheryl and Frank Beamer
Hello, Hokie Bird! by Aimee Aryal

Wake Forest University
Hello, Demon Deacon!
by Aimee Aryal

West Virginia University
Hello, Mountaineer! by Aimee Aryal

NHL

Coming Soon